THE TH1
"WE'LL MEET AGAIN"

Matt Wingett

THE THREE BELLES
STAR IN
"WE'LL MEET AGAIN"

Life Is Amazing

A Life Is Amazing Paperback

THE THREE BELLES STAR IN "WE'LL MEET
AGAIN"

First published in paperback 2012
by Life Is Amazing

First Edition

Copyright © 2012, Matt Wingett

ISBN 978-0-9572413-0-5

Acknowledgement: The author would like to thank
the Three Belles for their encouragement and pure
talent.
More power to you!

Please note, the characters in this book are fictional.
Any resemblance to any persons living or dead - except
for The Three Belles - is purely coincidental.

Dedication:

To my parents for being who they are, to Jackie for the same reason, to the countless friends who have encouraged me over the years.

To the old blind lady, Kathie, on the Isle of Arran. Without our chance encounter I would never have learned to write.

And, of course, to The Three Belles, for encouraging me to write this story, inspired by their 2011 appearance in Portsmouth Guildhall.

Meet the The Three Belles:

Betty – *Tall slim and blonde, Betty comes from a well-to-do family somewhere in the Home Counties. Betty likes horseriding and has travelled overseas during the hols from her boarding school. Betty is also known as Anneka Wass.*

Dorothy – *The daughter of a tailor from a little village in Devon, Dorothy is something of a mother figure to the Belles, loving to make do and mend, and supporting her friends through thick and thin. Dark-haired Dorothy has a modernday alter ego called Isabelle Moore. You should hear her rendition of We'll Meet Again!*

Gail – *from the East End of London, Gail has 4 brothers and 2 sisters. Her father is a stevedore on the Isle of Dogs and her mother takes in washing to earn a few bob extra. This vivacious, fun redhead with a twinkle in her eye and smile on her lips is known in some quarters as funloving Sally Taylor.*

1. The Lost Sailor

The more I look, the more exciting it gets! Bright, smiling blonde-haired Anneka surveys the audience for a few seconds more, then inhales a short, sharp breath and fires a grin at Sally. "This, I would say, is a success!"

The redhead beside her gives an excited jump for joy, her shining curls bouncing as she lands, her right hand clenched in front of her, a little fist of triumph.

"Oh, yes! I should say so!"

Their eyes drink the room. Sailors, soldiers and airmen mingle with WAAF officers, Wrens and ATS girls - and it's not only Forces attending tonight. Civvies in white cotton shirts, tweeds and flat caps, pin-stripes and trilbies add to the crush, as does a sizeable contingent of young women in flowerprint dresses.

On a table, the *Daily Mail* speaks of Russian vanguards closing on Odessa and of German retreats. The War-tide is turning. There's hope in the air. And the vocal trio called *The Three Belles* is making its Pompey debut in the Guildhall bar. *What a night to be alive!*

Dark, glinting eyes framed with sleek brown hair

approach through the crowd.

"Isn't it *spiffing?*" Izzie, the third *Belle*, tottering on tiptoes, her head back and her chin up, calls over the crush. "I never expected so many!"

"Tip-top," Sally shouts back.

A Home Guard drawn from Reserved Occupation in the dockyard sidles between Anneka and Sally, puts affectionate arms round their shoulders and says "Ready girls?" while an Able Seaman with a cheeky face chips in: "Your voices ain't gonna break my beer glass are they, ladies?"

Anneka flicks a raised eyebrow and gives an ironic smile. "It's all for the War Effort, you know." Then, hearing her chirruping mobile, she shrugs off the soldier and fishes in her handbag. The screen lights her face, her golden hair flaming ghostly white.

A text reads:

:-(

Soz cant make it!

:-)

Gd luk 2nite xxx

She thumbs a hasty reply - a smiley and a *X*.

A few minutes to go, she thinks. *All this planning and prep. 40s night. Props... music... costume. And to think we're being marked on this. Degree in historical harmonies. Notes of distinction, maybe? It's fun and an education. 'S life, really!*

Now they're ready. When the *Belles* break from the banter and nod to each other excitedly, the two ersatz heroes of the amateur dramatics society drift off to mingle with the audience *It's time.* Time to step into their 1940s stage personas: blonde Anneka becomes the flirtatious Betty, brunette Isabelle becomes kind-hearted Dorothy and red-headed Sally becomes the mischievous Gail. Fictional forties characters, they've scripted and worked up as part of their degree course. Their lecturers are seated in prime positions on the front row to mark the performance.

Bof-bof-bof. A slick young fellow taps a retro mic and announces:

"Ladies and Gentlemen, what you've all been waiting for. Please give a warm hand for... *The Three Belles!*"

The band strikes up - the audience cheers - and the classic 16 bar lead-in to *Chattanooga Choo Choo* fills the air with cupped *wah-wah* and carefree joy. Then *The Three Belles'* tight vocals wake an era gone by: a time of filmic poses, of tragedies and victories, of love and loss. Music flutters in the air, a dove of peace waiting to settle on the shoulders of the audience unconsciously leaning in - spellbound - misty-eyed romance.

The show's first half is a dream of tugged emotions. The seamless harmonies of the *Belles*: redhead, blonde, brunette, blending their old songs with appearances by guest singers and a comedian. A stranger, happening upon that crush of uniforms, those smiling women behind their mics, the military men with peaked caps pushed back, gals teasing, flirting, giggling, might think that maybe, just maybe, time has stepped backwards and snubbed the modern day. Magic fills the air.

The *Belles* conjure a *Boogie Woogie Bugle Boy Of Company B,* and *In The Mood,* concoctions infused with equal measures of joy and sadness. *Nostalgia, like a sweet bitter drug.* Then, as the audience's tears are pricked by the fake poignancy of blue birds over the White Cliffs of Dover, an air raid siren wails through the room like a mourning ghost, and serious-looking men appear, announcing: "Keep calm, and follow us please, ladies and gentlemen. Do not run."

They shepherd the audience to the "safety" of a smaller room where, lights out, a khaki-clad member of the am-dram cast strikes up an impromptu song by torchlight. *Knees Up Mother Brown, Don't Fence Me In* and *Lambeth Walk* - old songs that maybe once rang through the original Guildhall, before the incendiary hit it those years ago.

Grateful for the break, *The Three Belles* review the show and snatch a team-talk. Afterwards, Sally, laughing as ever, straightens up her red hair and reapplies some lippy, while dark-haired Izzie double-checks the set list. Anneka, turning to chat with the band's cornetist, is suddenly captivated by the sight of something - or more accurately, *someone* - on the far side of the room.

A melancholy figure gazes out through a window at the square below, with mute incomprehension. A sailor wearing the thick tunic and heavy sea boots of the Royal Navy, his tally cap reading only "HMS" to throw off the Enemy. He is young, in his twenties - *striking* - and blonde Anneka-Betty can't resist stepping over for a chat.

"Hello," she says breezily, approaching with a broad smile. "Are you all right?"

He turns to her as if in a dream. His young eyes have crow's feet around them, she notices, his face a look - *what is that he's playing? Worried? Haunted? Quite an expression!*

"Oh, yes, Miss, right as rain," he says without much force of conviction. "But you see, the thing is, I am trying to remember why I'm here..."

"Why you're here?" Betty-who-is-Anneka repeats, and gestures his get-up with an ironic wave of her arm. "Well it *looks* like you're in the right place! I have to say, you've gone to quite an effort!"

His eyes take her in for a moment, then he looks from her down at his uniform. A momentary struggle, hunting for words. "Really Miss, it's all a blank. A kind of darkness." He pinches his chin between his thumb and the crook of his index finger and goes quiet for a few seconds. "But if I remember rightly, I came here to see someone... yes... " he smiles suddenly, as a remembrance comes to him. "I've brought a surprise. A surprise for my gal."

"Well, that's marvellous," Anneka-Betty replies with a grin, glad the actor has found his way back into character again. *Like a blind man stepping in through his front door,* she thinks, *home at last.*

"My, you've got a lovely smile," he says. "Cheers me right up, looking at you does. Makes me think Al

Bowlly's right: *Tomorrow is a lovely day*. And you know, I think it will be. 'Specially after the surprise."

"What surprise?"

"I've got to give something special to my Betty... that's right. For Betts."

Anneka likes this. Character play; shifting identities. *Actors have the chance to be whoever they want.* She's intrigued and decides to help him along.

"Betty? That's me!" she laughs and sees his eyes settle on her with sudden intensity.

"It's *you*?" he asks, surprised. "Is it? Is it *really* you?"

"Of course it is," Anneka nearly laughs. *Shellshocked,* she thinks. *That's his character. What do they call it these days? Battle fatigue... PTSD.*

His eyes fix upon her, and in the middle of her thoughts, something descends on her, suddenly, like a physical blow, and her legs bend a little. An invisible weight she has to step back and support. She feels different, as if it's not only him who has stepped into that new coat, but that he has somehow forced her to fit in with his way of thinking.

It's like she's been cut down the middle and there are two of her now, fighting for control of her body. Two realities, one person.

She is inside the skin of another person, and has the bizarre impression of looking out at the world through a different set of eyes. She flickers between the two: for a few seconds she is modern Anneka, and then she is this other woman called Betts. *What is this?* Feeling like a puppet, directed by an external will that won't be denied, that makes her a double-act all in one. Her head spins, and she speaks her next words as if from a distance.

"So, sailor, where you headed?"

"That's censored Betts," he says, tapping his nose twice with his index finger and tipping his head forward and sideways. "Walls have ears, after all."

Oh, very good, modern Anneka thinks. *A little side-step to wriggle out of the details.*

He moves closer, eyeing her more intensely. Still haunted.

"My, it's been a tough old time, hasn't it, my darling?" he asks. There is something likeable - *vulnerable* - in the way he speaks. Somehow the *Betts* part of her two-woman show is touched by his warmth, by his humanity.

A flutter rises in her chest in response to his words. He is a half-remembered name, nearly recalled. *My darling! Have I met him before? Do I know him? Yes I do...* She is giddy with excitement, a flush in her cheeks, the hot joy of meeting him again, his familiar body, strong, known. She is under his influence, his spell. He goes on:

"I don't know how we cope, sometimes. Pompey, dear old Pompey's going to take more hits before this is over." He looks inwards briefly in quiet thought. A change of mood. Eyes seeking approval. *Confiding.* "You know, I heard that siren, and I reckoned I'd find you here, Betts..."

"Sireen?" she repeats. "Oh, siren, yes. Got you."

"Yeh. I knew I'd find you here at A.R.C. We've got to stick to it, Betts. We're dedicated, you and me. 'S why I like you."

Modern Anneka surfaces fully and considers him a little longer. *This is good,* she thinks. *After that false start, he's really in character.* But the thought is no sooner internalised than his iron will exerts itself and the other woman fights her way to the surface. Then, both Anneka and Betts seem to speak as one as they adopt a fake upper-class voice and coyly say:

"*Like me?* But really sir, we've only just met! What's your name, sailor?"

"Oh you *are* a one, Betts!" he says with a smile. "You know Freddie Budden's your sweetheart, Betts. Always will be."

He steps closer in, confiding something really meaningful, his eyes shining with his love for her. "I goes away tomorrow - and you'll still be here at A.R.C fire-watching. Well, Betts, let's see how good a fire-watcher you are. ...Look at my heart. It's burning for you!"

"A fire-whatter?" Anneka asks, the unfamiliar word jarring her back to the modern day for a moment. *Despite his oddness*, she thinks, *there is something about him...*

But through her other, older set of eyes, she is already under his spell. Warmth and sadness all at once.

Is he really going away? Can it be true? She wants to hold him, and laugh and cry, and block out the whole world and this stupid war, so it's just her and him, together. Then the modern woman fights her way to the surface again, like she is drowning, flailing between realities, and she looks at him with eyes of wonder.

He is brilliant at this! He makes me really believe I'm a different person. Who is he? She wracks her brains. *Local Amateur Dramatics? Maybe a professional? Right down to the scuff marks on his seaboots, and that Navy tunic that smells of fires, and war and the sea, he is so authentic!* The modern woman's thoughts break through briefly, before dying away in the static of her mind, and the spirit wireless retunes.

He says:

"I've got something special for you, Betts. What we talked about."

Betty gives him a flirtatious smile. She can feel her sadness mingle with expectation, a bitter-sweet principle in the blood, like dark chocolate and strawberries, like love and loss. "So... what exactly have you got for me, sailor?" She stands close to him with shining eyes.

"This, Betts," he says, pulling out a red leatherette-covered ring case, an oval of love. "Like I promised you." A *snap* reveals a little silver ring crusted with sparkling stones. His face grows serious. Without a pause he goes down on one knee.

"Betty, I would be truly the happiest man in the

world if you would accept my hand in marriage. Marry me Betts. Before I goes away to sea, let's get engaged!"

Delicious! - modern Anneka giggles with her Twenty-First Century girl's sense of irony. It's the laugh of a drowning woman, and then she has a thought she does not recognise as her own. *He's perfect! I love him!* Fluttering her eyes to the ceiling, she answers:

"Of course I will, Freddie!" She starts to giggle like a little girl as he really - *yes* - *he really does* - slide the ring on to her finger, handing her the jewel case to free both his hands and push it home. Her heart is all haywire, a UXB waiting to go off.

"Oh, thank you Betty!" he shouts with joy as the *all clear* wails around them, like relief exhaled. "You've made me so very happy!"

He stands, takes her in his arms and pushes his face towards hers, the rough feel of his woollen tunic beneath her hands, the smell of dust and grime and smoke hitting her nose. She leans towards him too, then suddenly, with a shock of realisation, Anneka surfaces fully from her dream. *Woah! This guy is seriously overstepping the mark.*

"Hang on a minute..." she pushes back against the wool, the hard press of his body against her hand.

A questioning look of incomprehension, mouth agape. He's about to speak when -

"We're back on!" an excited voice calls from behind her, over the sound of the *all clear.* "Come on Anneka!" Izzie-who-is-Dorothy is standing a little way off, and

Anneka steps away quickly from the sailor. Her hand jerks up to her temple and she eyes him with confusion. Then she glares disbelief at the ring on her finger.

"We'll talk about this later," she says severely, trying to work the ring off. "What do you think you're playing at!? ...Oh damn it, this thing won't budge." He is about to come back at her, but he's thrown by her assertiveness. "Later," she says, holding her hand up to silence him. "I'll speak with you later."

She turns and strides back towards Dorothy-Izzie, unconsciously dropping the ring case in her handbag as she goes, not aware of the look of confusion on Izzie's face. To her, it seems that where Anneka was standing by the window on that spring evening, a shadow has gathered in the shape of a man. She senses something dark... Something menacing... It is strange, but she allows it to pass under her conscious radar, in the way the half-noticed weirdnesses of the world go by unremarked. All she registers is a fleeting sense of fear, which she rejects in favour of her brighter version of the world.

"What was that about?" she asks, seeing Anneka's discomfort.

"Search me. Some prat getting carried away with his roleplay. Come on, I'll tell you later."

The *Belles* reunite as the hubbub of an excited crowd spills out from the "shelter" and the audience members find their seats for the second half.

The girls resume with *Don't Sit Under The Apple Tree.*

All is right again. *Betty, Dorothy* and *Gail* are in the flow of live performance - the heightened reality of the now - when there is no future and no past but everything gathers together into a single flowing eternity.

Yet as she sings, Betty occasionally remembers her strange sailor. She looks for him but cannot see him, and during the instrumentals she tries to work the ring off, turning from the audience to tug and twist it, until redhaired Sally-Gail steps over to her, leaning close.

"What's going on Annee-Belle?"

"This bloody ring," Anneka replies speaking to one side, her head down. "Some joker put it on, and I can't get it off. I'm meant to be getting engaged before the next number."

She raises her hand. Sally looks surprised at the silver band with its tiny stones glittering in the light.

"'That *is* rather posh," she says. Then, meeting Anneka's desperate look she adds: "Other hand." *Decisive. Always decisive.*

"What?"

"Use your other hand. It's a minor detail. No-one will notice. We'll get it off later."

Even as she is talking, Betty's stage sweetheart is tapping the lozenge mic in mock embarrassment.

"Ladies and gentlemen, I'm going to do something a little bit irregular, now. I want to interrupt this show to make an announcement."

He straightens and eyes the audience. *Get this right. Character has a certain posture. Pause for effect. Sense of seriousness. Embarrassment, too. Vulnerable.*

"You might well know that I've known Betty for some time now. I like to think that in the blackout, Betty and me, well, we've made a bit of light shine. She's a lovely girl. A *beautiful* girl..." *Pause.* "And I... well, Betty, there's something I'd like to say."

He pulls Anneka across the stage towards him. She smiles as he takes a ring case from his pocket.

"Betty, I love you. And if we can keep Gerry away long enough, I'd love to make you mine."

He kneels and looks adoringly into her eyes.

"Betty, will you marry me?"

Anneka-Betty looks around the room with a smile. *The icing on the cake! A lovely touch to play to the sentimental streak in the crowd.* She sees the faces of her friends, and the fans of *The Three Belles*, feels the charm the sentiment is weaving on the audience. Everyone knows it's a game, but even so, it's pulling them in. She holds out her right hand and laughing says:

"Yes! Yes, Kenneth, of course!"

A spontaneous cheer breaks out as he slips the ring home. Then he takes her in his arms, and they kiss. *More rapturous applause.*

In the middle of that stage kiss, Anneka-Betty opens her eyes and catches sight of the strange young sailor from earlier. He is scowling, a look of white rage in his eyes. She feels the hairs on her neck stand up, a shudder run down her spine. Her heart grows cold for a second. But then the crowd moves, and where his face was

21

there are just the smiling faces of the audience, and of the cast, gathered to congratulate her.

Anneka stands in the middle of the room in that stage embrace, wondering who the hell that weirdo was.

⚓

2. Under The Apple Tree

The after-show party goes on late into the night. After leaving the pub, a group of friends comes back to the big old student house the *Belles* share in Southsea for more drinks and chatter. Then, as the buzz dies down and they peel away, *The Three Belles* are at last alone together.

Sally, lounging on the sofa, gives a tired, satisfied laugh beneath her red hair. Her head is dropped back and the fine line of her nose points to the ceiling as she revels in remembrances of the show. Then, she sits up and she and Isabelle-of-the-dark-eyes press their shoulders close and huddle with a drink in their hands, savouring the moment and thinking of the future.

Only Anneka is quieter. As the deep night sinks deeper like a black pall over the island and the stars twinkle more brightly above, she detaches herself from the group and finds her way to the kitchen sink by the window. With a sense of annoyance, she begins to run cold water over that strange engagement ring. Then she soaps it and tries once more to work it off.

It is a problem, this ring, she realises - far more than

she imagined. Somehow, it seems to tighten on her finger, and the more she pulls at it, the tighter it gets. *Like it's glued there. My finger is sore!*

She intensifies the struggle, pulling at it over and again, but her fingers slip, and the ring will not move. She feels a sense of frustration rise up in her, and mingle with something else. *Panic.* Starting to whirl through her body. Then, her mind fills with a blur of thoughts, with the cold ache and the *sloosh* of running water and she hears a *tap-tap-tap* at the window. She looks up, startled, and sees... *a face!* A questioning look. He mouths something to her. She stares confusion, and for a split second sees her face meld with his in the glass, his features taking on for a moment her expression: bewildered and in pain.

Then he looks at what she is doing, and realisation spreads across his face. His expression changes. *Anger.* His eyes aflame: *frozen rage.*

She gasps at the force of that expression and steps backward from the glass.

"*Izzie, Sally!*" she shouts, reflexively calling out. They hear the fear in her voice and rush in from the living room to find her staring at the window, white as moonlight, pointing to the empty night.

"What is it?" Isabelle runs forward, eyes wide - "Anneka are you all right?"

"Someone out there - that guy - the one I told you about -" she says, and quick as a Spitfire fuelled on booze, Sally is out through the back door into the

Pompey night.

There is a dampness in the air, and Sally feels herself shudder deeply, unexpectedly, as the smell of something old hits her nostrils.

She walks towards the far end of the long garden, the tall silhouette of the Victorian house rising behind her against the stars. She steps under the cover of apple trees and suddenly it is completely black here - pitch, pitch black with a stifling closeness so that the air is like treacle in her lungs. She goes on, feeling her way with her feet, her hands out in front of her, eyes wide in the darkness, then stops and listens to the night. It is deathly still, and even the sounds of the city in the early hours, the soft *shush* of a car moving on the streets like a breath, the siren of a police car wailing on its way to attend a break-in or a fight, fade away. She shivers as she feels icy cold air enter her lungs, hears a movement nearby and a strange inhuman cry. She tenses for a microsecond, before realising that what she can hear is the barking of fox cubs in the garden next door, snuggling in the darkness, yelping under the stars for their mother to suckle them.

She turns on her heel and walks back down the path. She can feel her heart pounding, and is controlling her breathing to maintain composure.

Stepping back into the kitchen, she says: "I didn't see anyone. Nobody there."

Isabelle makes a pot of tea, and Sally joins the other *Belles* at the kitchen table, while Anneka explains what she saw. She tells them of the lonely sailor at the Guildhall, and shows them the ring again. She has already told them this in the pub, but now it is a different type of telling. It's not out of annoyance, or puzzlement. It's a telling from fear.

She describes how the strange sailor appeared again when Kenneth proposed to Betty. She recounts his look of rage. She shows them how sore her finger is from trying to get the ring off, and she tells them how the same guy appeared at the window, just a few minutes ago. *It was weird. It was scary,* she tells them.

With a fiery reply, Sally says: "Well, if I get my hands on him, he'll know about it!" - while Isabelle, more practically, says: "We should call the police. And for now, lock up." She and Sally make a circuit of the house, closing doors and locking windows, and call 999 to report a prowler.

Two police officers in reflective jackets turn up on bicycles twenty minutes later. Anneka gives them a description, and they go out into the leafy back garden with torches, only to come back inside after an exhaustive search, to report that they found nothing. Above the hiss and crackle of their radios, they advise the *Belles* to call them straight away if they see him again, and leave with reassuring words.

Anneka stands by the window, looking out pensively into the night, *obsessing,* Sally thinks, seeing her tense posture. *Best to make a joke of it:*

"If you see him, never mind the police - you tell me.

I'll give *him* a scare, all right!"

Anneka turns her head from the window and fixes her eyes on Sally. *Wide. Whites showing. Frightened.* "I don't want to see him again. Not one bit." Then she looks back out at the night, her eyes seeking the tiniest movement *in direct contradiction of her words*, it seems to Sally. She doesn't know what to make of it, and she shrugs at Izzie, who gives a shake of her head in return, her mouth turning down. Anneka stands there a while longer, seeming to see movements where there are none, and gazing absently at her own reflection.

Only when Anneka's phone starts to ring is the spell broken. She steps distractedly from the window and stoops to search in her handbag on the floor, pushing her long blonde hair behind her ear to keep it out of the way. As she extracts her phone she sends the leatherette ring case the sailor gave her tumbling end-on-end across the room. Isabelle picks it up to look at as Anneka takes a moment to read the display. *Will*, she notes, the man who played "Kenneth" - her fiancé at the show. *It's 3.17am, why on Earth would he ring now?*

Her phone log will record that she spoke with Will for eight minutes and 37 seconds, though it won't record her look of confusion and the intensity of the exchange between them. She asks him questions with a slightly frightened voice, and sometimes runs her fingers through her hair as she talks, asking further, almost breathless questions. And so it goes on, until she hangs up, looking more confused and tired than before.

The two other *Belles*, sensing something wrong, look her a question.

"It was Will," she says, knowing they know that already. "Sounds freaked out. He had this idea that a guy was in his room. A guy in a sailor's uniform. He said he was afraid for me. He couldn't explain why."

"An *idea?*" asks Sally, her voice rising on the final word, her face creasing. "What does that mean?"

"He doesn't know. He said he saw something that was like a dream, but totally real. He opened his eyes and there was a sailor in the room – or he thought there was - or something. When he sat up, the sailor left, slamming the door and knocking over a glass on the table outside. That bit definitely wasn't a dream... the others in the house heard the smash."

She looks around at the other *Belles* seated at the kitchen table, her eyes wide with fear.

"He can't explain why, but he's worried for me." She looks at the ring on her hand as she speaks. *Glittering, bright white metal.* "It sounded like it was the same guy who gave me this."

Sally crosses her arms in unconscious defence and, with her canine teeth, nibbles the inside of her mouth. Thinking. Gathering the information together into a picture. "So, there's a nutter on the loose..."

Anneka walks over to the table and sits opposite them, reaching across it to take the other two's hands in each of hers, as if she is feeling for warmth and normality. *Shaken up.* Their touch is calming.

"He said it happened about an hour ago. He didn't know whether to call me, but in the end he felt he really must." Then, she adds in a low voice filled with meaning, her eyes wide and her head low. "An hour ago is when I saw this guy. But Will's staying with friends in Petersfield. That's 20 miles away..."

The girls sit in silence for a moment, trying to make sense of this new information. Isabelle is the first to speak:

"Suppose there's something... supernatural about this?" she is voicing what Anneka has been unwilling to acknowledge. "My grandmother said there were always more things in the world than we understood... Presences..."

Sally shoots her a beauty of a look. "*Please*, Izzie-Belle... that's for horror movies."

But Anneka's attention is captured. "What do you mean by *presences*?" she leans forward.

"Spirits. Or maybe not. Memories that have stayed around. Grandma said some places absorb the memories of events. Do you think maybe our '40s night triggered something..?" She catches sight of Sally's bemusement, her head down and a one-sided ironic smile on her face. "Oh forget it!" she says.

"Izzie!" Sally bursts out laughing, then chides her: "You're going to have us believing in Father Christmas next!"

The redhead reaches forward and holds out her hand to Izzie with a nod at the jewellery box.

"Can I have a look at that?" She asks in a friendly voice. Izzie hands it over and her friend says: "*This* isn't very supernatural, is it? Maybe it'll have some clues about who this creep is..."

She turns the box over in her hand. *A neat oval. Musty smell of age*. She opens it to find, printed in the silk lining, a company name.

"Aha!" she says. "That's what we needed. See? From a real shop. Here. In Southsea. *J B Jackson, 4 Palmerston Road*." She gives the girls a steady look. "Tomorrow we go and visit. The shop's bound to have records. We give the jeweller a description of this guy, he tells us who he is, we let the police know, they go and have a chat and nip it all in the bud. Easy."

Her voice acts like a broom, clearing the dust from the girls' minds. The tension deflates from the room, and with a growing sense of calm, they bid each other goodnight, and peel away to their beds.

⚓

3. A Voice In The Dark

The sun is bright the following morning, picking out the whitewashed walls of the Thomas Ellis Owen villas and terraces on Kent Road as the *Belles* head towards Palmerston Road to chat with their jeweller. The faded grace of the old Portland Hotel shines in the daylight and branches rustle above, casting dappled shadows on their faces as they walk, picking out the neat lines of their figures. The night's drama has faded in the light and they chatter merrily, the lightness of their voices rising up and tangling in the branches like the wings of birds. Although Anneka gives a broad smile, something troubles her, that she doesn't tell to the others. The ring at times strikes a chill along her arm to her heart.

They turn into the top of the smart shopping centre that is Palmerston Road, with its little boutiques, scattering of hairdressers and clothing shops, and the sun shines more brightly still. *Morning heat*. The air is growing warmer by the minute as an early summer threatens to flutter in on the forked tails of swallows flown up from Africa, that nestle in the tall spire of St Jude's church.

They can't see a jeweller in Palmerston Road, and call at the library to ask. Nothing in the *Yellow Pages*, so they show the library assistant the ring box. A quick search online through the city records turns up a note that J B Jackson, bombed out in 1941, relocated to 78 Osborne Road. "Just round the corner," the librarian tells them.

They don't find a jeweller, but a little restaurant, filled with the smell of chips and beans, and the sound of frying. A bustle of people in for a Saturday bite before going shopping. Kids run around the *Belles'* legs, or bang with soft hands and plastic toys on the window, while exasperated parents do all the ineffective things they do when they're being run ragged. Among the clatter of cups and the *sheesh sheesh* of frying, they speak to one of the staff, a quietly-spoken man in his fifties with a bald spot and a fleshy mole under his right nostril. He eyes them blankly when they mention a jeweller, then remembers - *yes - maybe - a little further along the road...* And points with a fat arm.

Sighting a jeweller's at last, they note the name on the green-painted Victorian shop: *Valence and Co.* Inside, an elderly gentleman in tweeds greets the *Belles* and after a few questions, examines the ring case with curiosity. Anneka tries to remove the ring. Seeing that she can't move it, he acts to help her, with old-style chivalry and an experienced hand. But after failing to make any inroads, and catching Anneka's desperation, he suggests a jewellery saw. He is about to start cutting, when the ring suddenly comes loose and Anneka simply slips it off. *No effort whatsoever.*

"I can't believe it," she says to the room. "It wouldn't budge!"

The old man holds it up to the light and inspects the hallmark through an eyepiece, turning it over and admiring the workmanship, with a professional eye.

"It's lovely," he pronounces eventually, as he pulls the lens from his eye. "Really unusual. Hallmark 1940. Solid silver inset with little diamonds." He winks the eyepiece tight again and looks at it once more. "*Nice.* There's an inscription here." He angles it again. "*Betts, eternally, Freddie.* Tiny lettering, and perfect. And these diamonds... Whoever had this made in the war years had some money to burn - or cared a lot about this Betts woman."

"So it really did belong to a woman called Betts?" Anneka asks, an unexplained sense of foreboding gripping her.

"It's right there, inside," he replies, pointing with his little finger to its inner edge. "Fine, fine engraving. Good workmanship, like the ring."

Anneka looks distant for a moment. "That man last night. He called himself Freddie Budden. I remember it, now." She looks meaningfully at Izzie.

"What about the case?" Sally asks as the jeweller slips the ring into it. He hefts it and eyes it.

"An old design. This oval shape, that's the standard from a long way back. You know, new ones are usually square. They use plastic a lot these days, but this is wood. And the hinges are old - you can tell from the way they're finished, and they're slightly rusty, see? Nicely sprung, though, which is very unusual for a box of this age." He snaps the case shut with a *fap,* then springs it open again. "Nice piece of work..." He looks up at Sally, who is leaning in with curiosity. "As for J B Jackson... well I do remember there was a shop further along here. Closed somewhere around 1970. I wasn't even in the trade back then!"

This is as much as he can tell them. Of the jeweller J B Jackson, and the former shop, there is not a trace, and how you would track down the owner of that ring from 70 years before... no, he really can't help them.

The Three Belles thank him half-heartedly as they go. Outside in the bright air, they stop for a moment to think. Though the sun is shining, the day suddenly seems less bright and Anneka shivers, considering the welt on her ring finger that looks like some kind of burn. Even Sally's sparkle has temporarily left her eye.

It's then that Izzie turns to them by the Victorian shop-front with its curved glass stretching the reflections of cars puttering by, and announces matter-of-factly:

"It's time to see Aunt Isodora."

Blank looks from Sally and Anneka as she glides down Osborne Road a few steps ahead of them, in the direction of Old Portsmouth. She stops a moment and calls back at them with mock impatience.

"Well come on!"

⚓

Beyond the line of the sea wall in Old Portsmouth sits The Round Tower, the city's oldest defensive structure. A loop of narrow streets nestles beyond it, filled on its landward side with Georgian townhouses, post-War infill and 17th Century buildings that glimmer white in the sunshine and echo with the plaintive cries of gulls and the deep hum of ships ploughing the water. On the seaward side, crouching by the harbour mouth is a cramped line of brick and clapperboard buildings, where Izzie's Aunt Isodora lives in a flat, overlooking the rushing waters that empty from the harbour into the Solent twice a day.

They stand in the shadow of the street, smelling the sea air rushing up the road from Portsmouth Point, and consider the card beneath the doorbell they have just pressed. It reads:

Isodora Fay,
Spiritualist.

A hale matriarch in her 60s, short and sure-footed, with a wrinkled face, and a head of white hair packed with tight curls greets them. She gives her niece a long-time-no-see hug, placing her hands on Izzie's hips and taking a measured, appreciative look at her. After a few words, she shows them through to the rear of her house, opening the back door with a dramatic flourish and beckoning them to step through. There is no back garden, but a low pier stretching over the sea, with a small hexagonal hut at the end in mint green. Silently, she guides them towards it, the air swirling around them and the water gurgling beneath them as they advance over the deep green sea. At the hut, she turns to them, a serious look on her face, opens the door and shows them in.

The interior is all antique mahogany and smells of incense and beeswax, with little chairs around a green baize-covered hexagonal table. She invites them to sit, and tell her what has brought them here. She smiles at the girls encouragingly, and Izzie begins to tell their tale. As she goes on, Isodora notes of Sally *Not a believer, that's for sure!* But she forgets this in the concern she feels for Anneka. *She is wilting in front of me!*

Izzie's story over, Aunt Isidora says sternly:

"Well, my dears, you were right to come to me. There *is* something wrong with this, something very wrong indeed. I propose we contact the Other Side without hesitation."

"The Other Side?" Anneka repeats, a rising tone in her voice. *Alarm.*

"That's right dear. Nothing to fear. I have my guide to hand. He was once a Victorian schoolmaster... He's very kind. His name is Humphrey..."

Sally raises her hand to her face and coughs into a clenched fist to cover a snort of derision. She looks at the other two with raised eyebrows, *ridiculous* written all over her face. A sharp pain jolts up from her shin, and she looks a dagger at the dispenser of the little kick she has just received under the table. Izzie tips her head forward with fierce eyes, to remind her of her manners. A Paddington Bear stare.

Seemingly oblivious to the conflict, the old lady raises her hand dramatically, stares at Anneka for three seconds, then rolls her eyes upwards and continues. Her voice has a real tone of urgency about it:

"My dear, I sense something near you. Something that has followed you here and won't let you out of its sight."

She holds this pose a while longer, then gestures Sally and Izzie to pull down the blinds. The little boats and bigger ships plying the harbour disappear from sight, and the room sinks into darkness. Only the sound of the shifting water can be heard, slapping below, and the deep low vibrations of the ships passing by.

Next, there is a brief scrabbling sound, then a *shuk-chaa* as Aunt Isodora strikes a match, her face glowing golden in the blackness.

"Sorry for the drama," she says, playfully, her eyes twinkling in the flame. "I always forget to light it first." She locates the candle in the middle of the table, lights the wick, then shakes out the match, filling the air with a strong wood-smoke scent.

"Now, please join hands and look into the flame," she says. "Relax your minds."

Her eyes glint in the darkness as she fixes them with an intense stare.

"And I must warn you that whatever you see and hear over the next few minutes, keep your hands linked together, and don't be afraid. As long as you hold the circle, you will be safe."

The girls nod assent, though Sally does so with a kind of grim irony on her face. *What nonsense! What on Earth are we doing here?*

Aunt Isodora takes a deep breath, closes her eyes and gives out a low moan.

"My schoolmaster, my guide. It's me, Isodora, calling to you on the Other Side. Humphrey, are you there, my dear?"

A pause stretches out for a few seconds, and then Isodora slumps forward onto the table. Anneka, Izzie and Sally look at each other long and hard, and Sally is just about to speak when Aunt Isodora lifts her face again. Her features are contorted, now, in a strange expression of superiority. But this is not the thing that sends shudders down Sally's neck. No, it's not the look – it's the completely different voice. A voice unmistakably a man's.

"Isodora? Yes, I am here," it says, seeming to call from a distance, across a vast chasm of time.

Isodora replies in her own voice: "Ah! Humphrey... There you are. We have a question for you. A question one among us wishes answered."

Humphrey speaks again, eerie and deep: "I know it.

One among you brings a stranger with him. He is near you now."

The girls stiffen. Even Sally can feel her heart racing, although another more rational side to her is growing increasingly annoyed with this little performance. *How far will this woman push this?*

"A stranger?" asks Isodora. "Will the stranger speak with us?"

After a moment, the voice comes back:

"The stranger says there is one among you who is not of faithful heart."

"Will he speak with us?" Isodora persists. "I call on him now to speak with us."

The old lady falls forward again. Sally exhales and her eyes go up with exasperation to the ceiling. *Good grief!* Dark-eyed Izzie shoots her a warning look, and Sally does her best to bite her lip, while all the time, Anneka stares, spellbound at the woman across the table from her.

When Isodora sits up this time, she has a hurt look on her face. The voice she speaks in is one Anneka recognises instantly from the night before.

"It's me," he says, looking at Anneka through the old lady's eyes. "Me again. I saw you last night Betts," he says. "In the garden in that house. But you wouldn't let me in."

Anneka is staring back across the table with wide eyes. "It *is* you!" she says, clearly shaken. "Who are you?"

"Don't play that game. You know me, Betts. Freddie,

your old Freddie. I saw you last night, Betts."

"But why? Why did you follow me? Where have you come from?"

The room goes silent again for a moment. The sea splashes around the pier more violently than before, and the wind whistles through the woodwork, making the blinds rattle.

"Where from?" he asks. "I... I don't rightly remember. I just know it's been dark. Dark for a time. I've been alone, Betts. Alone. Waiting. Just waiting to tell you how much I want to be with you..."

Anneka looks at the other two girls with growing fear. The voice goes on.

"And here's the thing Betts. I came to tell you I love you. That's all. And then there's someone else on the scene. Someone you never told me about." Aunt Isodora chokes a sob in her throat. "You promised yourself to me. And then I see you with *him!*" Now the voice grows angry. "You promised yourself to me, Betts. I tell you now, I'm not going to leave you till you're with me..." The anger dies down in the voice, which grows frightened and lost again. "Oh, but my it's black in here. It's so black. Black as night."

The girls are unsure what to say, but even Sally is not grinning as ironically as she was when she sat down. Anneka is certain this is the same voice she heard last night, and Izzie, too, is sure they have their spirit, right there.

Aunt Isodora collapses on the table again, seemingly

40

exhausted. She takes a few moments to recover, and when she straightens up, to the girls' terror, something begins to manifest in front of her face. In the light of the candle, a semi-transparent shape begins to emanate from her mouth - a face seeming to float before them.

It's too much. Anneka screams.

Izzie stares with mouth wide open.

Sally acts.

Breaking the circle of hands, she takes the candle from the centre of the table and holds it up to get a better look at this new apparition.

Immediately it bursts into a crescent of flame, and Aunt Isodora gives out a scream.

"Oh shit!" she shouts, and stands up quickly, as the burning emanation flops on to the table.

The candle is knocked from Sally's hand in the panic and goes out with a little bumping sound, and the next thing, in the light of the flame coming off the apparition, the girls see Isodora swinging something towards them. The apparition goes out with a hiss and at the same moment, the girls are splashed with icy water.

Moving in the pitch black, Sally stands up and releases the blinds, which spring up quickly and flood the room with daylight. Aunt Isodora is trying to clear away from the baize table the charred remains of a piece of fine muslin, with a face painted on it. An empty vase stands on the table in a puddle of water.

Aunt Isodora looks up, livid. "I told you to hold your

hands and not break the circle!" she shouts. "You could have burned my face off."

Sally, her red fringe dripping, looks levelly at Aunt Isodora. She stops the old woman's ranting with a single accusatory finger pointed at the charred, damp cloth that the old woman had somehow hidden away on herself.

"That, I suppose, was meant to be ectoplasm?"

⚓

4. Retail Therapy

Before Sally raises the glass of G and T from the table, she gives the *Belles* an ironic grin and says: "Here's to spirits."

Bright sunlight is scattering bands of reflected light on the seawalls across from where they are seated at the Bridge Tavern, in the Camber Docks. Around the fishing boats wallowing on the oily water, the world is broken into a million moving facets. Sally goes on:

"I mean, *really!* Whoever heard of a spirit made of cheesecloth, or whatever it was?"

"Aunt Isodora... shame," Izzie replies, a little downcast. "Grandma always said she had the second sight." She sighs. "It's a disappointment, actually."

A stark image of the old woman makes Anneka laugh. "She was blue in the face by the time she had us out the door. I thought she was going to throw us off that weird pier... *You could have burned my face off!* Do you think she lives in that little hut?!?"

The girls laugh together, enjoying the sense of relief that is dropping through their bodies. In years to come this will be one to tell their friends, that's for sure.

As the laughing dies down, Anneka comes to a decision and she fixes the other girls with a determined look. "*Belles*, I think we've spent just about enough time on this, don't you?"

"What?" Izzie asks, surprised.

"Well, I had some weirdo approach me, but, you know, in the cold light of day, it all seems rather ridiculous. If he shows up, between us we will deal with him. But like this, we're letting him take over. I think it's time we got on with life. What's next? We haven't even talked about our little guest spot tomorrow, so a bit of planning for that. But most of all, I think we should be celebrating! Last night was a *success*, after all... I think we can safely say that our degrees are in the bag. And that deserves something, doesn't it?"

"Agreed!" says Izzie, her eyes sparkling in the light - "How about a bite to eat, to start with?"

"Yup, I'll go with that." Sally adds, with a little exhalation of relief.

None of the girls had realised how much this was playing on their minds. The shadow shrinks now, shrivelling in the daylight.

"And after that," Anneka announces, looking across to where the Spinnaker Tower and Gunwharf Quays beckon: "Shopping."

Raised glasses clink, drinks glow in the sunshine, and they let the warm summery wind blow away their thoughts of the night before.

They while away the afternoon trying on new dresses, picking a scarf from Marks and a top from Karen Millen - and slipping on shoes wherever they can. High-heeled red stilettos and low faun slingbacks, prim pink little numbers with pretty bows, and outrageous gold boots with zips up to their knees. There is nothing quite like it they realise: retail therapy with the girls. The joy of being out with the *Belles*, holding colours against hair and eyes, and laughing at the car crashes some of those clothes represent.

Then they take a trip to Albert Road, where the Vintage shops await. Old classics of design, and props for their shows, a fox-fur that looks so forlorn that the *Belles* can't help wondering who on Earth would have worn it. They find scarves and silk gloves and countless other little reminders of a world gone by, that make them smile at the style and coolness of those years past.

Back at the house that evening, they settle in the afterglow of the day in front of a rom-com from Blockbusters. Something starring Hugh Grant – light, innocuous and silly - all romantic nonsense, giggles and slush, that they allow to wash over them. They have their Doritos and a glass of red wine. *It's what life's about.*

They are about half an hour into the film when something in the storyline changes. A subtle shift at first, that when they look back on later, they will agree they cannot exactly pinpoint.

After that change, they find they are watching something quite different from what they'd expected.

The film that unfolds before them is like a dream, filled with the dark shapes of people running in the night, of the low phasing rumble of planes. And there is something strange about this film, because it seems to play on all their senses. There is the stench of acrid smoke, groundshaking explosions and the sound of bricks raining down with a highpitched *chink chink chink.* The tremors nearly knock the girls out of the sofa, and there are bursts of heat washing over them from the screen.

⚓

Interior shot: A sailor in a tunic and and tally cap tries a cell door from the inside and finds it locked.

Smoke is coming in underneath it and through the wicket. He grows increasingly desperate and begins to shout, hammering on the door over and over. More smoke comes into the room. He steps backward from it, looking around the room, wide-eyed.

Exterior shot: The Guildhall on fire. It's a blaze that shoots flames through the dome, the sound of molten metal whistling down to earth in glowing drips. The sky is criss-crossed with searchlights which light up barrage balloons; the constant sound of fire-bells and the at-at-at-at-at-at of heavy guns firing at night raiders. A singeing arc of tracer bullets flies upward in bursts of solid light, and then, even though it is just a movie, choking smoke fills the viewers' lungs. The Belles feel a need to retch.

Interior shot: POV of a person being covered with earth. Sinking down into blackness. The flames above seal away, closing to darkness. As if for a moment a gate has opened onto the pits of hell and closed again.

Scene fades.

At the end of this film, Anneka alone continues to watch another.

Exterior shot: A sailor stands before her and says severely: "You're mine now." He begins to lead her barefoot through the streets of Portsmouth, heading toward the Guildhall. She can hear its bells chiming around her, loud and sonorous, the old cry: Play Up Pompey, Pompey Play Up. The hour starts to chime with deep terrible vibrations that make the world shake, and the sailor takes her somewhere under the ground.

She gasps, closed in.

There is soil in her mouth.

⚓

She wakes into the bright dawn light, gasping for breath. All three are still on the sofa, staring as if they have somehow been drugged.

Around the breakfast table there is a tension in the air as each speaks of the strange film they watched, while the others follow along, noting every detail.

Afterwards, in the silence, Izzie gets up and checks the DVD. She shuttles through it, from beginning to end. *No war scene.* They check the tv listings, to see if they somehow watched another channel. Nothing meets the description. They look at each other, blearily surprised by the experience. It is "really weird" as Izzie puts it.

They all feel depressed, suddenly.

For Anneka, the last 36 hours are beginning to take their toll.

She is tired and drawn, and the welt on her finger where the ring once was is burning and puffed. She feels weak, as though her natural bright spirit is draining away and she slinks quietly off to the bathroom to put cream on her finger and to think.

But there is no relief from the feeling of dislocation that has been growing inside of her - a kind of fishbowl consciousness that makes everything out there seem like it is not her world. Everything is alien to her, she feels. As if this whole city is not her home, and never was. She rubs the cream on her finger hoping to take away the pain, but it stings all the more, and when she returns, she tells them about her movie with the sailor and the Guildhall, that the others did not experience.

When she finishes, Sally sits back at the table.

"Maybe it's psychological..." she says, musing out loud.

Anneka is interested: "In what way?"

"Well, you know, we've all got ourselves worked up about this weirdo, and it's having this strange effect."

Izzie shrugs. "I think there's more to it than that."

Sally looks her a question. "I might even be tempted to say you're right, Izzie. You think it's ghouls and ghosties... But we've already gone down that line, and we got *The Mystery Of The Flaming Cheesecloth* for our troubles. Maybe we should try something different..."

"Go on," says Izzie. "I'm open to anything."

"Well, if it *is* all psychological... the best thing to do is find out the truth. Blow our silly imaginations away with a good dose of hard fact."

"What do you mean?" Anneka asks. She sits back at the kitchen table and takes a long hard look at her redheaded friend.

"We put the pieces together and make a picture. What've we got? A sailor and the Guildhall. The sailor said something about it being used for monitoring air-raids or something. The next thing we've got is a woman called Betty, or Betts, who was a 'firewatcher'. Suppose we find out there's no truth in this at all? That way it's all just fairytales and bad dreams. - Which is what it is, by the way."

"But what about this ring? The jeweller says it's old," says Anneka looking down at the box on the table in front of them. "How does this fit in? Who are Betts and Freddie? What you're saying could be right, but *they're* not made up, are they?"

"We've got two names and a bit of a story. Our problem is we're filling in the gaps with our imaginations. Time to get proactive, instead of inventing worries for ourselves. We need to do some detective work."

Anneka likes the idea very much. "You're saying we start *The Three Belles Detective Agency*?" she says, with a little giggle.

"Exactly," says Sally, while Izzie joins in with a "Cool!"

⚓

5. ARP

That afternoon, the *Belles* have been asked to perform *a capella* at a celebration of the war years at the Groundlings Theatre in Portsea, an old converted school, not far from the Dockyard. Driving past the sleek line of *HMS Warrior* with a renewed sense of purpose, they agree the 19th Century warship looks *fab* in the water, and they smile again in the sunlight.

The Groundlings has a gorgeous feeling of light in the upstairs theatre. It's an 18th Century building of columns and arched windows. Kids are dressed in khakis, and grandparents and great grandparents sit and relive memories of the War and of everyday life in Portsmouth. After a reading from wartime editions of *The Evening News* and the showing of a short reel put together from vintage footage of the city, the *Belles* go on to perform, starting with *Don't Sit Under The Apple Tree* and *Lili Marlene*.

The thing about this part of Portsea is that the people cleared out by German bombs returned to the newly-built housing that went up in the reconstruction. Memory and place here are still stitched close together, like buttons on a Navy uniform, and the past is as real to these old men and women as if they lived through it yesterday.

When their slot is over, Anneka is approached by an elderly gentleman who tells them how much it brought back to him. He is called "Young Jim", he tells them. He was a *mudlarker* when he was a boy, and can remember the very first raid, when he was playing in the mud in the harbour. When it started, he ran in under the pier that supports the railway station over the sea.

"I remember, when the planes stopped bombing, we didn't think anything of it. We just got straight back out again and started playing in the mud. When you're a kid... well, you don't think of anything. 'Cept food, I reckon. Later on we had ice cream from Italian Tony who lived down our way. We called it hokey-pokey! It was a treat: the last ice-cream we had in the whole war, before the rationing came in, proper."

A jumble of remembrances spills out.

Remembrances of Portsea people proudly cleaning their steps and front doors, of the boys playing marbles in the streets because there were no cars, of lying on the chained logs floating in the harbour and catching crabs on the ends of little bits of string tied around little scraps of meat.

Fleeting moments of history: a man selling flypaper with a fly graveyard wrapped around his top hat. The cat's meat man who used to walk down the road with a cart followed by every pet in the neighbourhood. And running for the shelter in Saint George's Square, during an air raid.

"It was funny for me as a nipper," he says. "I just wanted to have the light on. You know, coz I was scared. But my ma, she was an ARP warden, and she, well, she really laid into me one time when I didn't do 'lights out'. I reckon I can still feel the stripes on my backside!"

He laughs at the memory, while Anneka suddenly grows more interested.

"Can you remember where she worked?" she asks. "What area?"

"Oh, I can do better than that!" he smiles. "I'm from a family of long livers, I am. You can speak to her yourself."

He shows her to where a shrunken old lady sits in the corner of the room, nearly bent double with age. Her face is a mass of lines and creases.

"This is my ma," he says, and then bends down to her, speaking clearly. "Ma... ma. There's a young lady here, she's interested in the war."

The old lady looks up and speaks to Anneka with a beaming smile. "You knows how to sing my love, don't you?" she says in a cracked voice.

Anneka smiles and sits next to her. The light coming in from the windows catches the old lady's face, and she smiles again with approval at the young woman.

"Thank you," Anneka says. "That's very kind."

"Now then my dear, what do you want to know about the war? I don't know if I can help you much...

Long time ago, weren't it dear..?"

"Your son, Young Jim there," she nods to him with a smile, "tells me you were an air raid warden. Tell me, where did you work?"

She sits back for a few seconds and looks into the middle distance as the cogs turn inside.

"Oh, a few places. I worked in this part of Portsea for a while. Then I got moved up to Landport when the bombs hit the house."

"Do you remember the raids?" she asks.

"Course I do. In the thick of it, weren't I? I even helped out at the control centre."

"Control centre?" Anneka echoes, suddenly uneasy.

"Up at the Guildhall before it were bombed out. Saw the Mayor there. He moved into the Guildhall so's he could take charge. A right old hive, it was."

"Were there a lot of people working there?"

"Oh, it were non-stop. We had people in the main hall, all sat in rows at desks, organising the city. They wanted me in coz of my little bit of secretarial training. Correspondence course from London."

"And that was all in at the Guildhall?"

"That's right dear. What did they call it? The A.R.C..."

Anneka feels her heart pounding with a growing, stifling fear. *Could it be? Could it be that there is something in this?* She looks up to see Sally and Izzie looking down on the pair of them, listening closely.

"Was there a woman working there? A woman called

Betts, or Betty?" she asks.

The old lady smiles for a moment and wracks her brain, sending the secretary with her correspondence course qualification back in time to check those old files in the back of her mind. After a while, she says:

"Betty? Yes, there was a Betty there... Except she was really called Elizabeth. Her name was... let me think... Betty Cheedle. That's what she was called. Betty Cheedle. It's funny, I got talking to a friend about her. She's over in a home in North End, last I heard."

"Betty Cheedle," Anneka repeats, with a smile, feeling suddenly lightheaded as she stands up. "Thank you, so much Mrs..?"

"Callow," she replies. "Mrs Annie Callow, young lady."

As she speaks, Anneka raises her hand to her temples and turns very pale, her legs weakening to jelly. She sways a moment, reminding onlookers of a wooden puppet on strings. Then her strength finally fails completely. As Sally and Izzie look on openmouthed, she buckles and plummets suddenly to the ground.

Only Sally's quick reactions prevent her from knocking her head as she falls senseless to the hard wooden floor.

⚓

6. Dead Ends

The journey in the ambulance to QA Hospital is a strange affair. It is cramped inside, and slightly unreal. There is a yellowness in the light that leaves Sally and Izzie feeling disoriented as they look with concern at the sleeping figure of Anneka. They touch their friend's hand from time to time, and note how cool her skin feels. She does not respond when the ambulance has to blare its siren, and there is not even a flutter in her eyes when they speak to her. She is breathing, tiny little spoonfuls of breath, and the paramedic looks at her undecidedly, asking her friends if she has been taking drugs - maybe a dodgy "E". But no, the *Belles* assure him that isn't the case, and he decides they look honest enough. He can't quite see a woman in forties gear getting out of her head to perform to pensioners at a remembrance of the Blitz, after all.

Anneka is admitted to a ward overlooking the island that stretches away from the south side of Cosham, revealing the low houses at its northern side interspersed with increasing high rises as the island reaches out toward the seafront. Sally and Izzie take a few seconds to look across the city. There is a mystery on that island. Both girls know it as they shift their gazes back to Anneka in her bed, to the city, then to Anneka again.

She is so pale, Izzie thinks. *As if she has sunk into herself, breathing with shallow short breaths. Is she going to be okay? What is it? Meningitis?*

After a while, the doctor and nurses who are watching her vital signs put an oxygen mask on her face. The doctor, an Asian woman in her late twenties takes a moment to look at her, puzzled. There is something unsettling about this young woman suddenly struck down.

With preliminary results coming back from the lab, and no evidence of a bug, the hospital staff start asking further questions. Might a poison have caused this? They take blood for analysis - but it's Sunday, and with staff shortages, the poisons unit will not open until tomorrow. It might take some time to run a whole series of tests.

After long hours of sitting and waiting with Anneka, Sally and Izzie leave glumly and catch the train back down to Portsmouth. Walking to Portsea to pick up their car, Izzie says sadly:

"So the story about the Guildhall being used as an Air Raid Control centre, that's true... What do you think about that, Sally? Do you think Annee-Belle's got overwhelmed by it all?"

Sally thinks for a moment. "I just can't believe she would be. And we're fine. I mean, it got into all our heads, not just hers."

Izzie sighs with relief at the admission. "Have you been thinking about this sailor business all the time, too? I can't seem to shake it out of my brain. Like it's taken control. I don't really understand it!"

"We're getting obsessed," Sally answers. "I'm starting to think there's some truth in the sailor guy's story. I'm beginning to think he really did know this Betty woman. Like he's a carer or a relative or something. And he's made this story up around her..."

"But why?"

"I don't know why! Because he's a nutter. Because he wanted to get close to a woman and poison her? He could have done something at the house, maybe with the food or something. Maybe there's something on the ring. We'll take it up to the hospital tomorrow."

Izzie is about to agree when her phone rings. She picks it up to hear an old lady, urgent and forceful.

"Izzie? Is that you Izzie?" The tone is tense and concerned.

"Aunt Isodora?"

"Izzie, listen to me. You need to find the real sweetheart. The woman this sailor wants to marry."

"I don't think we have time for this, really Auntie," says Izzie, glad to vent her frustration and concern somewhere. Aunt Isodora takes a deep breath at the far end of the line, and changes tack, quickly.

"That blonde girl. Your friend. She's ill, isn't she?"

Izzie is taken aback. She runs back over the call. Did she say anything to her Aunt Isodora about Anneka? No, she didn't.

"How do you know?" she asks.

"Izzie, Humphrey told me."

Izzie's shoulders drop forward and she gives a sigh.

"Oh, Aunt Isodora, don't start *that* again. We saw what your mediumship skills are really about. Bits of rag with faces painted on them. How are we supposed to believe you?"

"Now, young lady," says Isodora, turning assertive with her niece. "Listen to me. This is important. That trick I did with the cloth, that's something we all do, us mediums of the Old School. It's called a *convincer.* If your redheaded friend hadn't been so obviously sceptical, I wouldn't have thought of doing it."

"You wanted to trick us. And scare the living daylights out of us, too!"

"I am not having this argument, Izzie. We don't have time for it. Listen to me. Yesterday the presence I felt in the room was confused and lost. I couldn't get any real sense from it. So, I put on a show to add a bit of credibility to the proceedings. I'm sorry. I shouldn't have done that."

Knowing her headstrong old Auntie as well as she docs, Izzie realises that such an apology comes at a genuine cost to her pride. Mollified, she listens more closely.

"As well as being confused, that presence is angry, Izzie," she adds. "I'd say it's deadly. And all the more so because it doesn't know what's going on. You need to find the real sweetheart. She is out here, in our world. I have asked on the spirit plane, and no one has passed over connected with this spirit. The real Betts you are seeking can help this sailor see the truth."

"Yes, Auntie," Izzie says with a voice tinged with tiredness. "Whatever you say."

"Izzie, this is serious! Now, listen closely. I have had one piece of information from the Other Side. The person who can help you, she has a German name."

"No, I don't think so," said Izzie. "We know her name, and it is not German."

"Oh, will you stop contradicting me, you infuriating girl! You must find his real sweetheart. Find the woman with the German name. That is how you can help your friend."

After Izzie has told Sally about the phone call from Aunt Isodora, Sally fixes her friend with a level and rational eye. "That old fraud," she says. *Indignation.* "We know her name. Betty Cheedle. That doesn't sound very German to me!"

They talk through what to do next. Both are agreed that with Uni on vacation, and with visiting hours at

60

the hospital restricted, they need to do *something* to occupy themselves. Sally says:

"Suppose the guy Anneka saw was some looney who got this ring off his mother, Betts? And supposing she *did* work at the Air Raid Control centre at the Guildhall? Then he'd know a bit of background from her. If that is the case, all we need do is find this Betty woman, then we'll find this guy who is calling himself Freddie."

"Okay. Agreed," Izzie replies. "We've got her name, and we think she's in a care home on the island. Let's find her."

About half an hour into making phone calls, Izzie strikes gold.

"Betty?" says the care home worker at the other end of the line. "A nice old lady. Definitely from around here, yes. But I hate to tell you this... You've missed her, I'm afraid.

"Missed her?"

"Yes. You see, she passed on a few months ago."

Izzie is thrown, but she recovers from the surprise and says: "Oh, I'm sorry to hear that. I only called because I have something here I think belongs to her... tell me, does she have any children? Or grandchildren?" she asks, putting Sally's theory to the test.

The care home manager pauses briefly in thought. "No," she says. "She died very much alone, I'm afraid. No family to speak of, really."

"Did she ever mention the war?" Izzie asks. "Do you

remember her talking about it?"

"What a funny question! But no, not that I can think of. Some in that generation just want to put it all behind them. She never mentioned the war to me, not once."

Izzie puts the phone down and turns to Sally, who has a questioning eyebrow raised.

"Well?"

"A dead-end," Izzie says. "Literally."

⚓

Anneka has been walking through a fog for what feels like days. The land around her is featureless and dark - a marshy dampness underfoot that goes monotonously on and on.

"Hello? Hello..? Can anyone hear me?" she calls out, but the words are swallowed by the fog, and there is a kind of closeness in her voice that makes it sound like a stranger's.

She has no sense of direction, and no landmarks to guide herself by, but as she walks now she notices a change to the texture of the ground underfoot. Small stones make the marshy ground uneven, and then, suddenly, she is walking on a road. The fog takes on a thicker, more patchy texture, and ahead of her she sees a yellow-golden light. She steps on to cobbled streets, and notices bricks strewn on the floor. Uneven and jagged shapes of what seem to once have been houses, brick walls that are bowing and crumpled, as if a massive child has walked by and, with a petulant hand, smashed down the buildings. The wailing of someone in pain rises through the streets, and cries for help come to her from beneath the rubble. A muffled shout. A child crying. Above, she notices barrage balloons swaying slightly on their tethers in the blue sky, and here, down below, smoke and grime and dirt.

Ahead, a group of figures is gathered around a pile of bricks. Men in overalls and Royal Navy caps, working intensely, while a woman steps out from a terraced house with its windows blasted out, a tray of tea for the men. The smell of sewerage hangs in the air.

The men continue to work as Anneka walks up to them.

"Hello? Can you tell me where I am?" she asks. None of them respond. "Hello? Can you hear me?"

Still no answer. She waves her hand in front of their faces and they keep working, looking through her. She tries to touch one to get his attention, but his hand passes straight through hers. The world feels real, but the people in it, they do not see her or feel her.

"Oh my God," she says, a kind of shock charging her body. She feels a spin of fear and butterflies in her stomach and chokes back a tear, as she climbs on, over the pile of rubble. A pub has been cracked open on a street corner, and the landlord has chalked up a sign in the blast hole where a window used to be: "More Open Than Usual".

The people moving here are calling for silence as they listen for noises in the rubble, and she can hear the *tap tap tap* of someone beneath, knocking for attention. "There," says a police officer, pointing, and two sailors scrabble over an overturned Austin 7 in the direction of the noise, towards a jumbled pile of bricks, glass and household items - a mangle, a frying pan, a tin of brasso, and a miraculously intact china teacup among the wreckage.

She carries on, a siren wailing now, as well as the bells of police cars and fire-engines ringing in the distance. Smoke billows down through the tight little street, and she sees a figure she seems to know, watching her from a distance.

"Hello," she calls to him.

"Betts, you're safe!" He calls back. She recognises him.

"No!" she says out loud as he holds out his hand to her.

"Come, let me show you something," he says, taking her hand in his tight, cold grip. "I want your opinion."

From these tight little streets, she steps into more grey fog with this strange man. Suddenly, it is a different day with a very different feel in the air. It is dark, and there is traffic on the road with lights blacked. Trams are moving beside them in the darkness with their windows covered. They walk on for a while, passing a church on their right, and going down a busy commercial street.

She follows him as he leads her along another dark street, skittling through shadows beside the iron tracks of the tramlines, and stepping over cobbled surfaces. They stop outside a shop. People are walking carefully in the blackness, and a military car sputters by from time to time, just a sound in the blackness. The shop window has a board in the glass to blacken the night further. The board has holes drilled in to it, spelling OPEN in little pinpricks of light.

She pulls against his arm, but he just smiles to her. "I've been wanting to show you this for a long time."

They step into the jeweller's shop, the bell on the door ringing out sharply as they encounter a wall of black felt. He closes the door behind them, and then parts the blackout curtain. She feels different now, like a different woman. The shape of her body is longer and her limbs are more slender. She is hungry. Hungry all the time, she realises. *Rations.* They step into the cosy little shop and step over to the glass display case. An older man is looking at them from the other side.

In the display spread before them are rings on a black background. The sailor directs her attention to one ring. A silver band, studded with diamonds.

"What do you think? I know it's meant to be a surprise, but, well – I want to get it right for you," he says.

She wonders what this all means, and looks at him with a frightened smile.

"It's beautiful," she says in a voice that is not her

own. "But, Freddie, it's so expensive."

"Only the best for you, Betts. You know that." He puts his arm around her and kisses her on the cheek.

"Yes. Yes, Freddie."

"I knew it," he smiles. "I knew that's what you'd say."

The scene dissolves. They are on the steps of the burned-out Guildhall now. She can feel him tugging her along, and feels a deep sense of dread.

He leads her down through the rubble, down some steps to a flooded basement where the smell of smoke and ash and charred wood is thick in her nose. He goes on a little more, and finds a storage room further down, dripping with black water. At the back of the room the wall is loose, and bricks have fallen away. He pushes through the hole and pulls her behind him. There is clay all around them now, and it is dark, so dark. He pushes her to the cold ground and she feels his arms around her.

He does not let her go.

⚓

7. A Name From Long Ago

The following morning, the nurse at the end of the phone tells Izzie: "No change. She's still sleeping, and no sign of coming out of it." Izzie mentions the ring and wonders if she should bring it in - perhaps it is poisoned..? But even as she is saying these words, the idea seems utterly ridiculous. She is surprised when the nurse says: "Well, I think at the moment we are looking for *anything* to help us. So yes, bring it in. It *is* a strange rash on her hand, after all."

With nothing else to do, they have just got into their little red mini to drive to the hospital, when Sally gets a phone call from Young Jim.

"Sorry to bother you Sally," he says. "I got your number from the Groundlings. We've all been thinking about your friend. How is she?"

"Not so well, Jim, thank you for asking," Sally replies. "I'm quite worried, actually."

"Oh, I hoped she was over it. Well, maybe this isn't the right time," Young Jim says. "I don't want to be bothering you."

"The right time for what?"

"Just that - after your visit, Ma's remembered something else."

"Something else?" Sally repeats, sitting up in the driver's seat.

"Yes. About Betty. But maybe another time..."

"No, no, tell me more," says Sally, listening intensely now.

"Well, maybe it's best if you come down, and she can tell you herself."

The flat in Portsea where Mrs Callow lives is just around the corner from the Groundlings Theatre. It has a neat little courtyard with trees where, from a window on the ground floor, Mrs Callow often watches the children at play.

Sally and Izzie settle down opposite her in her living room, and Young Jim brings in a pot of tea for them, then says he will pop out. After asking after Anneka, Annie Callow explains that she had kept thinking about her question about Betty, because she seemed so interested.

"Now, my dears," says Mrs Callow, I have something more to tell you. There *was* another woman some of us called Betty. It was like a nickname. But most people knew her as - Katherine - Kathie."

"Do you know where she is?" asks Sally, feeling that they are closing in on the mystery.

"Where Kathie is? Why yes! She never moved. She's right here in Portsea!" The girls hear the door open. "In fact here she is now..."

A tall, elegant woman enters the room, ahead of Young Jim. She looks amazingly well for a woman in her late 80s.

"Hello," the newcomer gives a smile. She carries herself with a kind of dignity and uprightness, Izzie notices, and has a light airiness about her. "I hear you wanted to know something about the ARC in the war. I'm afraid I may not be able to help you. Unlike Annie here, my memory is all a fog, really."

After introductions are made properly, Kathie sits down with the little group and Sally begins to talk, excitedly.

"It's not really about the Air Raid Control centre, but about someone who might have worked there. We're trying to find out about a man called Freddie Budden..."

At the sound of that name, Kathy sits back in her chair for a moment and takes a breath, then sits up again, a curious look in her eyes.

"Freddie Budden?" she repeats. "Well, there's a name I never expected to hear again."

"So, you knew him?"

"Yes, you could say that," she replies cautiously. "But why do you want to know?"

"It's a long story, and we'll be glad to tell you. But a quick question for you: did he ever call you Betts?"

She eyes the girls, confused and suspicious. "No-one has called me by that name since he went away. Young lady what is this about?"

As Sally starts to spill out the story of the last few

69

days, Kathie's face displays a sequence of emotions. She moves from defensive, to curious to disbelieving to serious. When Sally is finished Kathie is silent for almost a minute, turning the story over and over in her mind.

"Is this some sort of joke?" she finally asks, looking at the two *Belles* with an intense mixture of anger and hurt. "Where did you get the name Freddie Budden? What are you trying to do? Upset an old woman with a student prank? How dare you come here, now, stirring up the past like this?"

Izzie and Sally are surprised by the reply and don't know what to make of it. There are tears in Kathie's eyes and her face is drawn and pale. Seized by an instinct, Sally pulls the ring case from her bag and snaps it open to reveal the jewel glittering inside.

"He gave Anneka this, in the Guildhall. It has an engraving on it. *Betts, eternally, Freddie,*" she says.

Kathie sits in silence as she takes in this new information. Then she bursts into tears. They seem to the girls to be very old tears. In fact, a lifetime's worth of tears. Annie Callow reaches for her friend's hand and gives it a comforting squeeze, and looks confusedly at the girls. It is all so strange, and not at all what she had expected.

After a while, Kathie takes control of herself and looks at the two women, her eyes reliving a long-dead past. "What does this all mean?" she asks, with a small voice. "What does it mean?"

"That's what we're trying to work out, Kathie," says Izzie, softly. "Who was Freddie Budden?"

Kathie takes a breath as she considers where to begin. Then she tells her story.

"Freddie, he was a dear. A lovely-looking sailor boy - and kind and sensitive, too. His eyes, when he looked at you, they made you feel special. It was true love between us. That's what I'd call it."

"What happened to him?" Izzie asks

"Oh, if I could tell you that, I wouldn't have suffered all this grief for these last 70 years!" she says, fixing Izzie with a painful look. "I've torn my hair out trying to find out. No-one knows. And my life, well, it's never felt right since he went. I suppose he was killed in the war, but they never found him. One day he was there. The next he wasn't. Years later I still thought... maybe he'll pop up somewhere. On the bus. In a crowd. Maybe I'll hear a knock at the door and in he'll walk. But he never did. And now, this. It's so very strange."

"What do you mean, no-one knows what happened to him?"

The girls see her eyes fill with memories, and the fog clears as she relives the past.

"He was a sailor, here in Portsmouth. At that time, when the bombing got worse, Admiral James, Commander-in-Chief at the dockyard, got Navy volunteers to help us civvies deal with the raids. I met Freddie at the Guildhall back when it was Air Raid Control. We organised firecrews, ARP wardens and sailors who'd been detailed to help us out. It was a hub. Freddie and me, we got to know each other. We laughed together so much. He was funny, but he was serious, too. And when we realised that - we'd fallen in love - he wanted to do everything right. He even took me to look at *that* ring," she points, "down in Southsea. Then, one night months later, he said he wanted to talk with me. I heard from a friend he was sailing out somewhere the next day. I had this terrible lump in my stomach, like a ball of lead when I heard that. I didn't want him to go..."

She pauses for a moment and gathers her thoughts a little more.

"I can remember his face in the crowd of working groups waiting to be detailed off at the ARC on that last night. It was the big air raid, and we just hadn't been able to find the time to be alone. January 10th 1941. That's when the old Guildhall went up. When we were evacuated, I lost him. I never saw him again."

She pauses now, the intensity of the moment fading away, her eyes clearing as she looks up at Sally and Izzie. "We had the Naval Provost come round looking for him a few days later. No-one knew where he was. But my heart was so broken, I somehow felt he was gone for good."

"And you're sure this ring is the one he showed you?" Izzie asks.

"Oh, that's the ring all right. Freddie promised it to me. He told me he was going to save every penny to get it, because I was his princess, so I deserved the best. I told him no, because there was a war on. You know - we should just get hitched... But he was a romantic. He wanted to do it right. There was no-one like Freddie."

She sighs, and runs her hand through her long hair.

"I eventually married someone else. Terry Mulliver his name was, an ARP warden in Pompey. He was kind to me after Freddie went. We had a good enough time, but I think Terry knew that no-one compared to Freddie, and Terry was sad about that. I found him sometimes alone. Just crying. It was like he was always trying to make it up to me. Trying to be Freddie. No-one could, you see. Even when he died, ten years ago, even then, I think he knew that he'd never been a replacement for Freddie. It was like he felt he'd let me down."

A question is burning in Izzie's mind, something that her Auntie said to her.

"Tell me, why did some people call you Betty and some people call you Kathie? Elizabeth *is* your real name, isn't it?"

"No. My first name is Beate. It was my Grandmother's name. It's Austrian. But you can't go around in wartime Britain with a name like that. So I became Kathie - which is my middle name. I was only ever Betty to people who knew me well, and only ever Betts to one man in particular. I didn't want everyone thinking, oh you know: *She's got a German name. She's a fifth columnist* or something..."

Sally and Izzie look at each other with some surprise.

So, Aunt Isodora was right!

Kathie looks at them earnestly. "But tell me, do you really think this is mixed up with all this business with your friend somehow?"

Izzie nods. "Yes, we think it is."

"But what do you think we can do? It's all such a long time ago. The ghosts of the past. I don't know how I can help you."

Sally sighs and looks to Izzie. With a kind of resigned sense of acceptance, she says: "No. But maybe there's someone who can."

⚓

Anneka wakes again from a fitful sleep filled with nightmares of another life – a life of meagre rations and dark streets in the winter. A life of strife and struggle, and make do and mend. And now she wakes into another nightmare. A voice whispers to her. It is a voice that speaks of love, and of kindness, but when she speaks back to it, it grows angry with her.

"I've been waiting so long. Why don't you love me? Why don't you speak to me right? We're meant for each other, you and me. You always said it. Freddie Budden is for you, Betts. Freddie is always."

It is dark here. Dark and cold. She can feel him pushing against her, holding her tight, his body pushed against hers as they lie in "spoons", on the wet earth.

Her eyes adjust to the darkness. It is as if they are no longer the eyes of a living person, but someone who is used to the dark spaces of the world. An underground creature. She looks down, and sees his hands clasping her. White. White like chalk. And the arms so thin.

She reaches down to touch them, to see if she can get them off her, and when she touches them her heart jumps. His arms are hard, like stone. She bends her head over her shoulder, straining in the darkness, and comes face to face with black eye sockets in a white face. An eyeless face, with white teeth grinning. White, white death in the blackness.

"You can't leave," he says. "You are mine."

She begins to scream at the sight of the skull, its dark eyes, its voice that comes from nowhere.

She thinks this must be a nightmare, but she does not wake up from it.

⚓

The Asian doctor looks down at pale Anneka in her bed. She notices, if it is possible, that she is even paler, now. Her breathing has become shallower than before, and her pulse is weakening.

She comes to a decision and strides over to the nurses' station.

"Nurse, call ICU. Her vital signs are deteriorating. We need her on life support."

She turns and looks again to the pale Anneka lying on the bed. It is bizarre. That's all she can think when she sees this healthy young woman, dying, for no reason at all.

⚓

8. Till I Come Marching Home

Aunt Isodora ushers the three women into her house, giving the slightly watchful Sally a nod of truce between them. She does not take them out the back to the hexagonal hut, but into her front room, where there is a large table with a candle burning in a bowl, and neat furniture with pictures from the Victorian era on the wall. Kathie looks around this strange room with uncertainty as Isodora bids them sit, then pulls the heavy black curtains closed.

Aunt Isodora turns from the darkened windows, gathers her thoughts for a few seconds and addresses the group:

"This spirit I have been trying to contact - it – *he* - is lost. The task has been difficult. His memories are scattered and he isn't sure what or who he is. But he does know that he has been searching for the woman he loves. That person, whom he thinks is your friend Anneka," she turns from Izzie and Sally to Kathie," is in fact you." She looks closely at her. "Kathie, or Betty - or Betts as he knows you."

She pauses a moment, to impress upon the women

there the seriousness of what she is about to say next.

"Some strange things are going to happen in this room in the next few minutes." She shoots a sideways glance at Sally. "I need you to be open-minded."

Kathie, Izzie and Sally give a nod, and Isodora continues:

"I need your help to call this spirit and to manifest him. And I really do intend to bring the apparition into our reality from the Other Side. It has long been known that strong emotion can do that, and the burning strength of raw emotion I have encountered in my contacts with him make me sure that he will manifest, here. Emotion is a kind of lens... And love, is perhaps the strongest emotion of all."

She puts her hands up to a little silver cross around her neck, and eyes it for a moment with distraction, seeking safety in its charm. Then she drops her hands by her side and sweeps her eyes across the faces of the women, like a searchlight, or the beam of a lighthouse, warning of a wreck.

"You must be aware that he is moving in half-light and shadow, and is confused. He cannot make his world make sense. To be honest, I don't know what he will do. But we need him to move on and find peace. Only that way will he release the spirit of your friend," she nods to Izzie and Sally, then looks to Kathie again. "We need you to show him the truth, Kathie, to help this spirit to understand."

Kathie freezes for a moment, uncertainty playing on

her face.

"But if he thinks she is me, what will he do... to me?" Kathie asks.

Isodora looks at Kathie briefly, and says: "Love is strong, Kathie. We need you to show him the truth." She takes a breath and continues: "Join hands on the table please. We are going to call him. Call him now."

As Isodora sits with the group, and begins to talk, her face goes blank. Her voice is soft and calming, and she mutters ramblingly to herself. Little snippets of conversation, whispers and sharp orders issue from her lips. It is as if she is talking with a whole group of people that the others cannot see. Some she dismisses, some she questions – asking the same thing over and again. "Bring me this sailor. Bring him to me."

Then, as the minutes go by, she sits upright, the candle spreading little shadows on her face, and making her features shift and change. It is as if a hundred other people have entered the room, and inhabited her body. Her face is serious now, her eyes open. She is staring ahead. She seems to recognise someone, a shadow in another world. "There you are. If you can hear me and you wish to talk, give me a sign."

There is a long silence in which the women can only hear their own breathing. The silence stretches on and the candle gutters a little, then comes back again, as bright as before. Sally pulls a face, and Isodora fixes her with a fierce stare.

"Wait!" Isodora hisses. "Wait"

Then there is a knock against the wall. Sally can feel the hairs on the back of her neck stand on end, as the temperature in the room drops. When she exhales, she can see the ghost of her own breath in the candlelight.

Isodora says:

"Welcome, sailor, welcome. Now understand this: we want to help you. Believe us, we want to help you."

Then, a voice speaks out of Aunt Isodora's mouth, the same voice that they heard on that previous visit.

"Help me? How can you help me?"

Kathie gives a gasp then sits back in her chair, stunned at the sound of that voice. She knows it well, even after all these years. Isodora continues:

"There is one here who knows you. She wants to speak with you." She nods to Kathie. "Speak now."

In a frail voice, plaintive and self-conscious, Kathie says: "Freddie? Freddie? It is me... Beate... Betts..."

The candle goes out with a fizzle. There is a silence for five slow seconds. Then the room erupts in an explosion of violence. A vase crashes to the floor and the desk in the corner of the room topples over as if an unseen figure is having a fit of rage. The women hear Isodora's voice over the crashing noises. "Stay calm. Keep your hands connected. Maintain the circle and he can do you no harm!"

Izzie feels Sally's hand squeeze her own, hard, while she in turn keeps a tight hold of Kathie's. A whirlwind moves around them, and items in the room are caught up in them, again and again.

"What's this trick?" Freddie's voice calls in the dark. "What are you up to?"

The candle in the middle of the table re-ignites and wells up into a massive jet of light, and Isodora calls again:

"Hold your nerve. Stay calm, ladies..."

The women look around in horror at the brightly lit room. Objects are moving, catching the firelight, glinting spinning. A black vortex, gathering up more and more items, tugging at the women's hair. A sense of deep, malevolent anger bears down on all of them. They can't breathe.

The shoots higher and higher, blackening the ceiling and threatening to set the room alight. Already it is licking at the lampshade above them. They can see - with vivid intensity - the fire spreading across the ceiling, sending sparks down upon them.

Frightened by the inferno, suddenly Kathie shouts:

"Freddie! If that's you, stop this. What are you doing?!"

A black, malevolent whirlwind veers out of the room, the door slamming behind it. The women are left in a ponderous silence as they sit catching their breaths. They are shaking. Izzie is breathing tight little gasping breaths. There is no fire, they see. It was an illusion. No fire at all.

Sally takes charge of herself despite the adrenalin rushing through her body.

"Well, that didn't quite go according to plan," she

says, and is immediately cut across by Aunt Isodora with a warning voice.

"Shush!" She is staring into the distance. "He is coming. He is coming nearer again."

On the street outside, they can hear the sound of slow footsteps approaching on the paving slabs. Stepping nearer, the clomp of heavy boots on the flagstones. The steps stop just outside the front door and there is a silence for thirty seconds. Then they hear three slow knocks at the door.

Isodora raises her head. "Enter! Come in you poor lost sailor. Come in."

The handle squeaks and the front door creaks as it swings open. Then they hear heavy bootsteps in the hall that stop outside the living room door.

Isodora is impatient, now. "Come in. Come in."

The handle turns and the door opens. All the woman stare up to see that the space in the doorway is unoccupied. *Nobody there.*

But Kathie does see someone. In the doorway, she sees the sailor as clear as the last time they spoke. Memories flood in. Tears fill her eyes.

"Freddie, is that you?" she asks. The other women are aware now of an icy coldness in the room, and an area of darkness by the door. Kathie, however, sees his expression, his clothes, the way he moves, the way he stands. The fear on his face.

"Freddic! Are you all right?"

From the darkness a voice sounds in the room.

82

"Who - who is that? Who is that?" he asks, his uncertainty making his voice quake. He is silent again, and the dark air moves closer to the old woman, slowly, hesitatingly. "Betts... Betts... Is that you? My God, what's happened to you? You look so old."

She reaches her hand up to the empty air and puts her palm flat against what might perhaps be a face.

"It is me, Freddie. It's me."

She takes an unseen hand and puts it on her neck. There is a silence, then a puzzled voice says:

"You look like her, but you can't be her. Are you her grandmother? Who are you?"

"It's me. Freddie," she says with a voice of resignation at the years that have piled up on her, and not on him.

A chair at the side of the table pulls back, and they hear the creak of leather as he sits beside her.

"It can't be you. Betts. Can it?"

"Freddie, my love. So much time has gone by, but I remember it all like it was yesterday."

"It was only three days ago, Betts. During the raid. I heard the sound of the Air Raid warning and wanted to come looking for you. I have what I promised you. A ring. We, we are going to get married..."

The voice pauses, trying to add together the sight of the old woman, and all the things that have happened in the last few days.

"I think I must have been hit by something. I woke up and everything's different here, now. Everything's changed in Pompey. There's all these funny looking cars on the roads, and whole streets have been wiped out. My God!" A realisation comes into his voice. "My God! Oh, God..."

She looks at him. "I lost you in that raid Freddie, and I never saw you again. And the years have gone by, and I looked for you and hoped to see you again, for so long. So long. And here you are. But I never dreamed... not like this."

There is a silence for a minute that feels like an hour.

"Now I understand. I'm..." The voice dies away, and there is the sound of his sobbing. A deep, sad sobbing.

Kathie looks at the others around the table. "Please leave us," she says. "We need to speak, alone."

Isodora nods to Sally and Izzie, and the three of them stand to leave. As they step out of the door, the women turn around and see a figure, the shadow of a man, like the memory of a dream when the waker wakes, reaching out to touch the old woman, and holding her in his arms - and they hear the sound of two people weeping – weeping at the injustice of the world, at the life a young sailor never had, and the pain of the years in between.

⚓

Sally and Izzie notice that there is a spring in Kathie's step as she leaves the room after her talk with her lost sailor. She moves more lightly on her toes, like a woman whose years have fallen from her. There is a look of peace in her eyes, and a smile on her lips. Aunt Isodora welcomes her with a gentle hand, and asks her to sit.

"Does he understand?" she asks. "Does he understand that he can't make time turn backwards?"

Kathie nods. "He does," she answers. "The truth was that he had no idea. He was just lost and confused, and trying to make sense of what he knew. He had been asleep a long time."

"Asleep?" Izzie asks.

Kathie takes a breath and is contented. "He was killed in the raid. That's all he would say. It seems he's been waiting for me all this time. He gave me this."

She holds out her hand with a smile to reveal that she is wearing the glittering silver engagement ring. Sally, surprised, looks in her bag, to see that it has gone.

"I told Freddie that I'd got married to Terry Mulliver, and that he had been good to me. I told him we'd had kids, and the life we'd led. I told Freddie, too, that even though Terry looked after me, I still hoped Freddie would come back. I never forgot him."

"And what about Freddie? How did he respond?" asks Aunt Isodora, earnestly.

"He understood it all. And more so when I told him it wouldn't be long. I told him: *we'll meet again*."

With a voice of urgency, Izzie asks: "And did – did he say anything about Anneka?"

Kathie looks to the two young women. "Yes, he did.

He said you should go to your friend. And he said something else."

"What, what did he say?" asks Sally.

"That he understands now and that things are clear. And he is sorry."

⚓

9. Nor The Centuries Contemn

Anneka is standing at the Guildhall. It is Armistice Day, and a service is being held at the War Memorial. The crowd is respectfully listening to the words of the priest. Then, as the time draws near, a bugler sounds the Last Post. The Guildhall clock strikes 11 o'clock and the crowd falls silent for two minutes. At 11.02, a cannon reverberates across the city from Whale Island. When the service is over and the crowd disperses, she walks to the War Memorial - a line of piled poppy wreaths, little remembrances in blood red, spilled on the monument steps.

Around her are the names of so many killed in the war, and she takes a moment to consider them, reading along the rows of names, and then sitting for a moment in the quiet curve of the memorial, a magic circle in the cold breeze.

As she sits, wrapped up in her thoughts, she doesn't notice the figure who shuffles up and stands a little way off from her. But suddenly she feels a deeper coldness in the air, deeper than the cold that the winter has spread around her, and she smells a smell that speaks of age, and earth and something terrible that was once in her dreams but has long since gone.

She takes a sidelong look at the figure and recognises the worn seaboots and the dark tunic.

"Don't be afraid, Miss," says a familiar voice that makes Anneka's hair stand on end. "Don't be afraid."

She looks around her and realises that none of what she can see is real. It is a strange, hovering world, a febrile and see-through unreality in which she is moving.

A faceless figure, a dark presence that is both there and not there all at once hovers near her. He is no longer clear as she saw him on that first night, nor deathly and angry as she once sensed him to be, but a strangely inhuman figure, one that is transforming - in the process of preparing to migrate to another place. A few moments go by before he speaks again.

"I came to say sorry, Miss. I really am. I couldn't remember, you see? I heard a sireen wail, and I thought it was the night that I last saw my gal."

"The last time you saw her?" Anneka repeats, wondering what he can mean.

"That's right, Miss. I couldn't tell you before because I couldn't remember it. But it's all come back to me now. The last time I saw my Betts."

Anneka bridles at the name, feeling her breath catch in her throat. She has the urge to stand and walk away, but realises that this world is not hers. That he is in control of it.

"There's a reason I was never reported as killed."

He pauses a moment, and when he speaks again, his voice is earnest, almost pleading. "Miss, there will come a time soon when I will need your help. When it will be time for me to pass over."

"My help?" asks Anneka, the fear still pumping round her body.

"Yes, Miss." The figure raises a hand – pleading and placating all at once. "Now hear me out. You will understand. On the night I went missing, I told one person I was about to propose to my Betts. He was an ARP warden who knew her, too. When he heard me say what I was going to do, he seemed to go all funny on me. Then, out of the blue, he invited me down into the old police cells beneath the Guildhall. He said there was something he wanted to show me - that he'd uncovered it in one of the raids, and didn't know what to do with it. I wasn't sure what to make of what he said. So I followed him. But it was all a dodge, Miss. A rotten dodge."

"A dodge?" Anneka repeats, half intrigued and half revolted by this ghastly figure.

"He wanted to get me alone, see? And when I wasn't looking, he knocked me over the head. I swear if I'd seen it coming, it would have been him and not me. But I didn't see it coming. And when I came round, the door to that cell was locked. That warden who'd done it to me, how was I to know he held a secret flame for Betts? He just wanted her for himself, see? When I told him I was going to propose, he must have got the brainfever or something, coz he thought we were rivals in love. Of course, someone would have let me out if they'd known I was there. But then, that couldn't happen. Not that night. I look at it now and realise he couldn't have known that Gerry would raid like he did. But Gerry did raid, and the place went up."

He pauses a moment, reliving those final minutes of his life: "When I woke up and smelt the smoke coming in through the door, I just tried to hide. There was a wall at the back of that old cell where the bricks had all come loose, and behind it was another little alcove. I went back there, you see. To get away from the smoke and the flames."

The figure is agitated now, the voice in anguish. "I didn't last long. I felt the heat, like a furnace down there. All the air went from the place. And that was me. Finished."

He pauses a moment, overcome with sorrow and with the pain of remembrance.

"Even when they rebuilt the Guildhall. They missed me, see? They missed me. Hidden in my alcove, tucked under the walls."

The figure moves closer now, leaning over Anneka, the gap where his face should be a dark pit, a whirl of blackness. She recoils, but his body language is kindly and his insistent voice tells her he is eager for her to follow him.

"I need to show you, Miss," the spirit says.

Anneka shudders with horror, but at the same time she is curious and she knows she must follow him. A few minutes later, two people wander in past phantoms of sight-seers and people having their lunch in the Guildhall café. She follows the figure down the stairs to the cloakroom under the Guildhall, where once the cells lay.

At the front of the cloakroom is a long wooden counter with a line of racks behind it. Further back, through a door is another room, and in that room is a set of steps going down to yet another door.

She recognises this place with a shock to her heart. Her legs go weak. But the faceless figure waits patiently, and she finds her strength and carries on.

At the far end of the room is a wall. The plaster here has started to crack, and when he puts his hand on it, the bricks fall away to reveal a hole. He steps inside, and she looks into the darkness for a moment.

She takes a breath, a whirl of fear spinning up through her guts and making the palms of her hands tingle. She ducks in through that crack in the wall. Behind her, she hears the door to the underground room close with a *clunk*.

It is dark.

She stands shivering in the cold, her eyes beginning to adjust to the lack of light. She can make out a strange whiteness, lines of white against the darkness, almost glowing.

It is a horribly familiar scene. His bones. His bones

are there, and the remains of a tunic, trousers and sea boots, half rotted away, the white lines around the collar showing in the dark.

Beside these remains, the ghost of Freddie Budden is standing. The voice speaks again:

"The man what done this to me... His name was Terry, Terry Mulliver. He married her, Miss!"

The voice cracks for a moment, then carries on. "He married Betts. Oh, that's the truth of it!" He goes silent a while, as if in an internal battle, before he goes on.

"But here's the thing, see: Betts don't need to know this. I don't want nothing upsetting her now. She lived her life with him. She had kids with him. She don't need her heart breaking twice by someone finding me, and lots of newspaper stories, and maybe, somehow, the truth getting out. But, there will come a time when I have to sleep proper, like. The fact is, I need a decent burial, Miss. That's what I'll need you for."

Anneka stares at him and then at the bones on the ground. What can he mean? Before she can ask, he says meaningfully:

"You won't remember now, but you'll know when the time is right."

The scene fades to nothing, and a new one appears. She is walking blindly, she realises, and has been doing so for some time. There is a fog again around her, and she is calling for someone to help her. She can't quite work out what has happened. One moment there was the darkness of that room, and the voice of a stranger telling her something, and the next there was just grey fog. She walks on, over ground that is no longer strewn with rubble. The floor is soft, she realises. She notices green grass growing underfoot, and lightness spreading around her. There is a brighter patch of light ahead of her, lighter than the rest of the fog, and she walks toward it, her body warming, as if she is in sunlight – like a leaf unfurling on a spring day.

She carries on, feels the warmth grow more, and can hear a steady rhythmic gasp, like the exhalation of a steam train. She thinks she is coming to a railway station, from the sound of it, a station that she is not sure where its passengers leave for. But still she can see nothing.

Now the greyness around her has turned to a kind of red-brown, and the sounds seem realer than they did before. She walks towards the light again, and realises that she is looking at the insides of her eyelids.

There is light shining through them. She opens her eyes, and sees a bright light above her, and can hear the sound of machinery working to pump something, something organic that depends on machinery to survive. There is an antiseptic smell and a pair of eyes looking down at her. The Asian woman's eyes study her with kindness.

"Welcome back," she says, with a smile. "Welcome home."

⚓

Six months after Anneka is released from hospital, she receives a telephone call from Aunt Isodora to say that Kathie died peacefully in her sleep. The funeral is due to be held the following Thursday.

The other *Belles* are away. Sally is on holiday with her boyfriend, and Izzie is visiting relatives in the North. As a mark of respect, Anneka decides to attend the funeral at Milton Road Cemetery, on the east of the island, without her two friends. She sees Young Jim there, and Annie Callow, who both nod to her kindly and approach her afterwards. Annie says: "She didn't want to be cremated. She said there had been enough fire in her life." And the two invite her back to a friend's house nearby to drink tea and eat sandwiches with the dwindling band of friends and relatives - all that is left of the War Generation.

After it is over Anneka drives down towards Old Portsmouth, sweeping along the seafront, and considers how it was when Kathie was young: a tangle of barbed wire and concrete blocks with guards patrolling the Front near the pier. She sees the line of blocks that were the old submarine barrier stretching away into the sea, and imagines the girls of the ATS crew, handling the anti-aircraft guns at Southsea Castle. She feels she can remember another's memories - the bustle of the streets, their darkness, the buses with their windows painted for blackout, the people migrating to the country every night to avoid the bombings. They are memories she owns now, borrowed from another.

She stays that night at Aunt Isodora's, who is happy to put her up, and lying awake, she looks up at the clear sky above the city, and sees the black infinite, and is filled with a sense of wonder and sadness, before she falls asleep. It is a peaceful sleep, with the sound of the sea in her ears, and the ferries and boats ploughing through the water.

When she wakes, she thinks a little more about the War, and the fun she had running a night's entertainment at the Guildhall when all this started. Reacting to an unexplained whim, she decides to take a walk by the Guildhall, stepping up through the streets of Portsmouth on a cold winter's day. As she goes, she considers the previous six months. Things are going well for *The Three Belles*. They are gigging regularly, and appearing at shows and forties events. She owes a lot to those soldiers and sailors and airmen and women of the forces, she realises, in more ways than she has considered before.

At the Guildhall, a large crowd has gathered around the square, and with a feeling of growing supernatural fear her skin begins to crawl with recognition. Her palms are sweating and she feels as if she is moving in a dream as she approaches the group of people there.

It is Armistice Day, she realises, and a sense of

unreality steals across her as she watches the crowd listening to the priest. A bugler plays the Last Post, and the clock strikes 11 o'clock as it did in some dimly remembered dream. She stands stock still, as if she and the rest of the city have been trapped in amber - as if time itself has wound down. In those two minutes of silence, parts of a dream come back to her. She has experienced exactly this before, and she knows exactly what will happen next, just before it does.

At 11.02am a cannon echoes across the city from Whale Island and after a while the service comes to an end. With her growing sense of *déjà vu*, she feels compelled to walk to the War Memorial. She sees a line of piled poppy wreaths, little remembrances in blood red, spilled on the monument steps.

Just as she experienced before, she notices the names of those killed in the war in Portsmouth, and she takes a moment to consider them, and what this *déjà vu* might mean. She reads along the lists of names, and then sits quietly for a moment in the quiet curve of the memorial, a magic circle in the cold air.

She remembers the words of the service she has just heard, which take on a fresh meaning:

They shall grow not old, as we that are left grow old:
Age shall not weary them, nor the years contemn.
At the going down of the sun and in the morning
We will remember them.

She has her own, private, minute's silence.

It is as she sits there that a figure in dark clothing

walks near her, and she feels a sense of deep terror. *It's a loop,* she thinks. *A loop in which I'm caught, maybe forever.*

She looks down at the black boots the man is wearing, then, taking a hold of herself, looks up, expecting to see a blank space where a face should be.

A policeman is standing by her, a young constable, looking at her with some concern at her apparent fear.

She understands now. She knows what to do. Freddie's sweetheart has passed over, and he, too, is ready to go. He needs to be buried. Laid to rest. Smiling, she stands, and looks at the young policeman.

"Hello there," she says to him, speaking with a clear voice.

Then, to his surprise, she says: "I need to report a death. You might call it a murder. It happened over 70 years ago."

He takes a step back from her, wondering what to make of this assured young woman who smiles at him and stands, pointing a directing hand towards the Guildhall. "It's this way..."

And to his puzzlement, she adds in explanation: "It's important we don't forget him."

⚓⚓⚓

A Personal Message From The Author

Thank you for reading this book about my home town of Portsmouth. I hope you liked reading it as much as I liked exploring the streets of Britain's only Island City and letting my imagination roam.

★

And of course, if you liked it, please recommend it to others!

★

About The Three Belles

You can find out more about this talented trio on their facebook page (just look up The Three Belles) and on their website, thethreebelles.com.

★

I have written other stories based in Portsmouth, and am intending more for the future.

Please look out for the following titles, which are available as e-books:

Turn The Tides Gently
Heaven's Light Our Guide
The Tourist
The Tube Healer
The Boiler Pool

★

Connect With Me Online

Twitter: @TurnTheTidesGen
Facebook: https://www.facebook.com/matt.wingett
My blog: http://www.mattwingett.com

★

A Final Thank You

Finally, I'd like to say *thankyou* to Paul McKenna. Yes, the hypnotist and personal development expert. In April 2008 I was attending a training course in Neuro-Linguistic Programming with him. At the time I was suffering a loss of belief in my writing ability that was so pronounced that I just couldn't write any more.

Paul demonstrated a hypnotic technique on me, and it unlocked my writing after years of stagnation. The first things I wrote after this were admittedly enthusiastic but crude - but Paul certainly did something to me that I have worked on ever since.

So, Paul, thanks for that. You gave me the ability to get back in touch with my creativity, and for that I am grateful.

⚓